HOUSTON TEXANS

BY TOM GLAVE

Published by The Child's World®
1980 Lookout Drive • Mankato, MN 56003-1705
800-599-READ • www.childsworld.com

Acknowledgments
The Child's World®: Mary Berendes, Publishing Director
Red Line Editorial: Editorial direction
The Design Lab: Design
Amnet: Production

Design Element: Dean Bertoncelj/Shutterstock Images
Photographs ©: Tom DiPace/AP Images, cover; Andrew
Dieb/Icon Sportswire, 5; John Amis/AP Images, 7; Pat
Sullivan/AP Images, 9; Icon Sportswire, 11; Eric Gay/AP
Images, 13; Aaron M. Sprecher/AP Images, 14–15; Patric
Schneider/Icon Sportswire, 17; David J. Phillip/AP Images,
19, 21, 29; Ric Tapia/Icon Sportswire, 23; Rich Kane/Icon
Sportswire, 25, 27

ISBN 9781631439957
LCCN 2014959700

Printed in the United States of America
Mankato, MN
March, 2016
PA02312

ABOUT THE AUTHOR

Tom Glave grew up watching football on TV and playing it in the field next to his house. He learned to write about sports at the University of Missouri-Columbia and has written for newspapers in New Jersey, Missouri, Arkansas, and Texas. He lives near Houston, Texas, and cannot wait to play backyard football with his kids Tommy, Lucas, and Allison.

TABLE OF CONTENTS

GO, TEXANS!

The Houston Texans are not the city's first football team. The Oilers played in Houston from 1960 to 1996. But the owner moved the team to Tennessee after the 1996 season. A new owner wanted football back in Houston. He worked hard to make it happen. It finally returned in 2002. Fans were thrilled. They filled up the stadium right away. Let's meet the Texans.

Running back Arian Foster (23) stretches for the goal line in a game against the Dallas Cowboys on October 5, 2014.

WHO ARE THE TEXANS?

The Houston Texans play in the National Football **League** (NFL). They are one of the 32 teams in the NFL. The NFL includes the American Football Conference (AFC) and the National Football Conference (NFC). The winner of the AFC plays the winner of the NFC in the **Super Bowl**. The Texans play in the South Division of the AFC. They have never won a Super Bowl. Houston has been to the playoffs twice. They lost in the second round both times.

Gary Kubiak led the Texans to their first winning season in 2009.

WHERE THEY CAME FROM

The Oilers left Houston in 1996. Bob McNair wanted football back in the city. He started working toward it in 1997. The city agreed to build a new football stadium. The team would share it with the Houston Livestock Show and Rodeo. Houston was awarded an **expansion** team on October 6, 1999. The team was named the Texans a year later. Houston played its first game in 2002.

Owner Bob McNair is a big reason why the Texans brought NFL football back to Houston.

WHO THEY PLAY

The Houston Texans play 16 games each season. With so few games, each one is important. Every year, the Houston Texans play two games against each of the other three teams in their division. Those teams are the Indianapolis Colts, Tennessee Titans, and Jacksonville Jaguars. The Texans also play six other teams from the AFC and four from the NFC. Games against the Colts are especially tough. Indianapolis is often the best AFC South team.

The Texans and Colts often battle for the AFC South crown.

WHERE THEY PLAY

The Texans play in NRG Stadium. It opened in 2002. NRG used to be called Reliant Stadium. It was the first NFL stadium to have a **retractable** roof. NRG holds 71,500 people. The Super Bowl was played there after the 2003 season. College football games and soccer games are also played at NRG. And it is still the home of the Houston Livestock Show and Rodeo.

NRG Stadium has been the Texans' home since they entered the NFL in 2002.

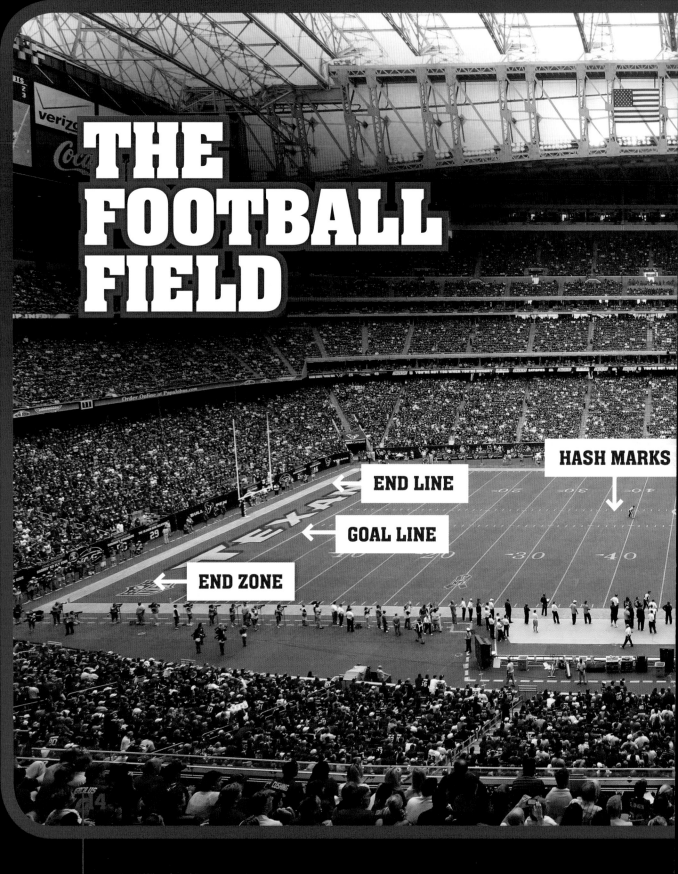

THE FOOTBALL FIELD

END LINE

GOAL LINE

END ZONE

HASH MARKS

SIDELINE

GOAL POST

MIDFIELD

20-YARD LINE

BENCH AREA

15

BIG DAYS

The Texans have had some great moments in their history. Here are three of the greatest:

2002—Football returned to Houston on September 8. The Texans beat the Dallas Cowboys 19-10. A sellout crowd filled NRG Stadium. No expansion team had won its first game since 1961.

2011—The Texans won the AFC South. It was time for the team's first playoff game. Houston met the Cincinnati Bengals on January 7, 2012. The Texans won 31-10. Defensive end J. J. Watt returned an interception for a **touchdown**.

Wide receiver Andre Johnson (80) and his teammates celebrate a touchdown in Houston's first playoff win.

2012—Houston won 12 games and the AFC South. It won two **overtime** games in five days. No other NFL team had done that. The Texans met Cincinnati in the playoffs again on January 5, 2013. And once again Houston won.

TOUGH DAYS

Football is a hard game. Even the best teams have rough games and seasons. Here are some of the toughest times in Texans history:

2005—The Texans went 2-14. They should have won a third game. Houston led the St. Louis Rams 24-3 at halftime on November 27. But the Rams outscored Houston 24-3 in the second half. The Rams won in overtime.

2007—The Texans played the Tennessee Titans on October 21. Houston trailed 32-7 after the third quarter. The Texans made a furious comeback. They led 36-35 with 57 seconds left. But Titans kicker Rob Bironas had a great day. He hit a **field goal** as time expired. It was his eighth of the game. That was a record. Tennessee won 38-36.

Defensive end N. D. Kalu looks on in disappointment after Tennessee Titans kicker Rob Bironas's last-second field goal on October 21, 2007.

2013—Houston was coming off two playoff appearances. But this season was a disaster. Star running back Arian Foster missed eight games due to injury. The Texans started 2-0. But they then lost 14 straight games.

MEET THE FANS

Texans fans love to **tailgate**. A local store runs a contest for the best tailgate at every home game. Houston's biggest fans sit in "The Bull Pen." It is located in the north end zone. These fans lead the crowd in cheers and songs. Toro is a blue bull mascot. He wears a Texans jersey. *Toro* is Spanish for "bull." The Texans have at least one "Battle Red Day" each season. The players wear special red jerseys. Many fans also wear red on those days.

Houston fans love to wear the team's colors when supporting the Texans.

HEROES THEN

Quarterback David Carr was Houston's first draft pick ever. He played with Houston for five years. Matt Schaub replaced Carr. He led the NFL with 4,770 passing yards in 2009. Linebacker DeMeco Ryans led the Houston defense for six years. He was the 2006 NFL Defensive Rookie of the Year. Defensive end Mario Williams made the Pro Bowl after the 2008 and 2009 seasons. Wide receiver Andre Johnson was drafted in 2003. He led the NFL in receiving yards in 2008 and 2009. He made seven Pro Bowls with Houston before leaving the team after the 2014 season.

Quarterback Matt Schaub led the Texans to their first two playoff appearances in 2011 and 2012.

HEROES NOW

Defensive end J. J. Watt is one of the NFL's best players. He had 20.5 sacks in 2012 and 2014. That made him the first player to have at least 20 sacks in two separate seasons. He was named the Defensive Player of the Year both those seasons. Watt salutes the crowd after sacks. He also wags his finger after knocking down a pass. Running back Arian Foster is awesome. He led the NFL with 1,616 rushing yards in 2010. He led the league in rushing touchdowns that year and again in 2012.

Defensive end J. J. Watt (99) celebrates after sacking New York Giants quarterback Eli Manning on September 21, 2014.

GEARING UP

NFL players wear team uniforms. They wear helmets and pads to keep them safe. Cleats help them make quick moves and run fast. Some players wear extra gear for protection.

THE FOOTBALL

NFL footballs are made of leather. Under the leather is a lining that fills with air to give the ball its shape. The leather has bumps or "pebbles." These help players grip the ball. Laces help players control their throws. Footballs are also called "pigskins" because some of the first balls were made from pig bladders. Today they are made of leather from cows.

Wide receiver Andre Johnson played with the Texans from 2003 to 2014.

HELMET

SHOULDER PADS

GLOVES

THIGH PADS

FOOTBALL

CLEATS

SPORTS STATS

ere are some of the all-time career records for the Houston Texans. All the stats are through the 2014 season.

PASSING YARDS

Matt Schaub 23,221

David Carr 13,391

RUSHING YARDS

Arian Foster 6,309

Domanick Williams 3,195

TOTAL TOUCHDOWNS

Arian Foster 65

Andre Johnson 64

RECEPTIONS

Andre Johnson 1,012

Owen Daniels 385

INTERCEPTIONS

Dunta Robinson 13

Marcus Coleman, Aaron Glenn, and Johnathan Joseph 11

POINTS

Kris Brown 767

Arian Foster 392

Defensive end J. J. Watt (99) became one of the NFL's best defensive players soon after joining the league in 2011.

SACKS

J. J. Watt 57

Mario Williams 53

GLOSSARY

expansion when a league grows by adding a team or teams

field goal a method of scoring worth three points in which a player kicks the ball between the goal posts

league an organization of sports teams that compete against each other

overtime extra time that is played when teams are tied at the end of four quarters

retractable something that can be pulled back

Super Bowl the championship game of the NFL, played between the winners of the AFC and the NFC

tailgate when fans gather outside of the stadium before a game to picnic around their vehicles

touchdown a play in which the ball is held in the other team's end zone, resulting in six points

FIND OUT MORE

IN THE LIBRARY

Edwards, Ethan. *Meet Arian Foster: Football's Ultimate Rusher.*
New York: Rosen Publishing Group, 2014.

Gilbert, Sara. *Built for Success: The Story of the NFL.*
Mankato, MN: Creative Education, 2011.

Stewart, Mark. *The Houston Texans.*
Chicago: Norwood House, 2013.

ON THE WEB

Visit our Web site for links about the Houston Texans:
childsworld.com/links

*Note to Parents, Teachers, and Librarians: We routinely verify our Web links to make
sure they are safe and active sites. So encourage your readers to check them out!*

INDEX